# Christmas
# Animal
# Tales

# Christmas
# Animal
## Tales

Illustrated by Caroline Pedler

**Stripes**

STRIPES PUBLISHING
An imprint of Magi Publications
1 The Coda Centre, 189 Munster Road, London SW6 6AW

A paperback original
First published in Great Britain in 2007

ISBN-13: 978-1-84715-027-1

A CIP catalogue record for this book is available from the British Library.

Printed and bound in Belgium by Proost

2 4 6 8 10 9 7 5 3 1

# CONTENTS

# FUZZY

Adèle Geras

Annabel was longing for Christmas. Christmas Eve was a week away and today was the last day of school before the holidays. The children had spent days and days making decorations to put up in the classroom, and there were paper chains looped over the windows and a big tree in the corner by the nature table, which was hung with stars and glittery balls and tinsel in pretty colours.

The best decoration of all was the big picture stuck on the wall above the bookshelves. Everyone had helped to make it and they'd only finished it yesterday. There was a fireplace in the picture, with red and green stocking-shapes hanging off the mantelpiece, ready for Santa Claus to fill with gifts when he'd popped down the chimney. Everyone could see Santa was coming, because there were his black boots, just visible in the background. Each child had chosen something special to make and Mrs Bowen had made sure that every single thing was firmly stuck to the paper. Kevin had cut out some golden stars and you could see them in the window. Parveen had coloured in some paper mince pies and these were glued to a paper plate and arranged by the fire. Some people made ornaments, some made chairs and tables, and others made toys to lie around on the floor in front of the fire.

When the children were choosing what they wanted to do, Annabel's hand went up first.

"Please, Mrs Bowen, can I paint a picture of a cat?"

Everyone laughed. They all knew that Annabel was cat-mad and she liked ginger cats best of all. She drew them on scraps of rough paper; she used orange paint to put a cat into every single picture; she played cat games with her friends at playtime and they said:

"Why don't you get a real cat?"

Annabel wrinkled her nose. "I keep asking my mum and dad," she told them. "They say: 'all in good time'."

"What does that mean?" Holly wanted to know.

"I don't know," said Annabel, "but I think it might mean 'no'. "

"Of course, Annabel," said Mrs Bowen. "Let's make a really splendid cat for the picture. Look at what I've got for you."

Annabel went over to see what Mrs Bowen had found in her box, the one she always called a treasure-chest. This box was full of scraps of shiny satin, soft velvet and glittery gauze. There were balls of wool in sugary colours, ribbons and braid and lace and scarves and sequins in packets and a roll of cotton-woolly white fleece fabric that was going to be very useful at Easter. Mrs Bowen told Annabel, "We'll have a field up there on the wall in the spring, and you can all make lovely white lambs to go in it. But just for now, we're Christmassy, aren't we, Annabel, and we need a cat to sit by the fire and wait for Santa. Look at this."

"It's beautiful!" Annabel smiled. She looked at the square of fabric, which was a sandy kind of orange. "I'd love a ginger cat. I'd love a cat that was exactly that colour."

"Yes, dear. I know how you feel about ginger cats. Let's cut out the shape and you can stick the whiskers on and put the cat in the right place."

"Can my cat have a ribbon round its neck?" Annabel wanted to know.

"Of course. You choose the colour."

Annabel chose a special white Christmassy ribbon that had tiny red holly berries with green leaves on it.

When the cat-shape was ready to stick on to the picture, Annabel added the ribbon, which was now tied in a bow, and glued a few black pipe-cleaners to the cat's face.

"I'm going to call my cat Fuzzy," she said.

"It's not your cat," said Kevin. "It's the class cat."

"But I made it. And I'm going to take it home with me for Christmas, aren't I, Mrs Bowen?"

"We'll see, Annabel. For the moment, we want it in the picture. All your mums and dads will be coming in to see what we've made, when we have our carol concert tomorrow."

Before the carol concert, Annabel took her mum and dad to see the class picture.

"Look!" she said. "That's my cat. That's Fuzzy. Isn't he sweet? Stroke him. See how furry he is. I wish I could have a real cat just like him."

"What a lovely picture!" said Annabel's mum, stroking Fuzzy and then moving on to look at something else. "I think you're very clever, all of you. And Fuzzy's really life like, isn't he?"

On Christmas Eve, Annabel and her little brother Henry helped their dad to get everything ready for Santa.

"Mince pies!" Annabel told Henry. "Santa loves mince pies."

Mum had put four on a plate and Annabel placed this near the chimney. "You can't light a fire in here tonight," she said to her dad. "Santa's boots would get singed as he came down the chimney."

16

"Righty-oh," said Dad, pouring a little sherry into a glass and putting it near the mince-pie plate. "He'll need a sherry, I think, don't you? After all that riding about in the sleigh that he does."

"Henry!" Annabel shrieked. "Look, Dad, Henry's eaten one of Santa's pies! You're naughty, Henry. Very, very naughty."

Henry grinned and Dad said, "Never mind, Annabel. He's just a bit greedy and he's only a baby. Don't look so worried. We'll get another pie for Santa."

"I wish I could have brought Fuzzy back from school with me," Annabel said. "Mrs Bowen said I could have him after the holidays. In the New Year. But I wish he could come to our house for Christmas."

"Never mind, dear," Dad said. "It'll soon be school time again and then you can bring Fuzzy home. He'll be fine in the classroom till you get back, don't worry."

Annabel sighed and decided to think about tomorrow. There would be lots of presents and delicious food and Granny and Grandad were coming for lunch. And the mince-pie plate and the sherry glass looked just right. She was ready for bed now. The quicker she fell asleep, the sooner Christmas morning would be here.

When Annabel woke up, it was still dark. It must be the middle of the night, she thought, because Henry was still asleep and he always woke up very, very early in the morning. She could hear a noise, coming from downstairs. What was it? It sounded... no, it couldn't be, could it ...? It sounded like a kitten, miaowing. She got out of bed and tiptoed to the top of the stairs. The door to the lounge was closed. The noise was coming from the kitchen. Did she dare go downstairs on her own? The landing light was on, because Henry was scared of the dark. Annabel wasn't really scared because she was a big girl, but she liked the light on as well.

There was a big, box-like thing on the kitchen floor by the radiator. Annabel came closer; the miaowing noise was definitely coming from it. Could it be? She knew what cat baskets looked like and this was a cat basket, she was quite sure. It was bigger than any other basket she'd ever seen and it had a little window cut out of one side, with wire bars across it. You could see in, though, and Annabel held her breath as she bent down to have a look. When she saw what was in the basket, she cried out, "A ginger kitten! Oh, it's a real cat!"

She sprang up, wanting to tell someone, but everyone was asleep. What time was it? She went into the hall to look at the big clock and saw that it was nearly five.

"It's you, is it?" said Mum, leaning over the banister on the landing. "I heard someone walking about. I thought it might be Santa."

"Mum! There's a kitten in the kitchen. Have you seen it? Did you bring it? Was it Santa?"

Mum came downstairs and gave Annabel a hug. "No, that was us, I'm afraid. Santa doesn't do big cat baskets. A thing that size would never fit down the chimney, would it? And cats aren't all that fond of reindeer. Dad and I had to fetch Fuzzy ourselves. From Mrs Gradwell, down the road. Her cat had a litter of kittens a few weeks ago."

"Why didn't you say anything?"

"We wanted it to be a surprise on Christmas Day. Well, that hasn't quite worked out, but never mind. It's Christmas Eve."

"Can I call him Fuzzy?"

"What do you think? Dad and I have been calling him that ever since we saw your lovely cat in the classroom picture."

"I love him," Annabel said. The miaowing had stopped. "He's asleep, I think." She went over to the basket to check. "Yes, he's all curled up. He's so lovely."

"I'm glad you like him," Mum said.

"Now how about coming upstairs for a bit more sleep yourself?"

They left the kitchen together. Annabel knew she wouldn't be able to sleep, but she didn't mind. She decided to lie in bed and think about Fuzzy and all the fun they were going to have together.

# A HOUSE FOR
# A MOUSE

Michael Broad

It was Christmas Eve and Lucy's parents were tucking her into bed. They kissed her goodnight, turned out the light, and were about to leave the room when she sat up and frowned.

Lucy was a bright girl who was at the age where she'd started asking questions, big questions like, "What does the tooth fairy do with all those teeth?" And from the look on her face, her mum and dad knew she was about to ask another.

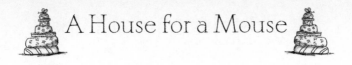 

"Is Santa Claus really real?" she asked. "Or do you go to the shops and buy my presents instead?"

Lucy's parents laughed and admitted that they sometimes helped Santa with some of the gifts, but that he was still absolutely, definitely real. Then they exchanged smiles and secret glances.

Grown-ups are often unaware that their children see everything, and Lucy saw the smiles and secret glances. But she accepted their answer and lay back down again.

"We'll see," she whispered, because Lucy had a secret of her own.

Unlike most children on Christmas Eve, Lucy didn't feel the need to gaze out of her window for a glimpse of Santa's sleigh. Come morning, she would know whether he was real or not.

So, she closed her eyes and fell fast asleep.

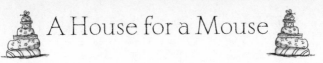 

In the street below Lucy's window, a tiny mouse was waking up. He poked his nose outside the crisp bag that was his home, and looked around cautiously.

The mouse didn't know it was Christmas, but he knew something was going on. Over the last few nights twinkle lights had appeared in the windows of the houses, there was extra food in his regular bins, and now snow was falling everywhere.

He thought the snow looked very nice, but the cold nibbled his feet.

The mouse had also noticed that families were gathering together, and as he shuffled from his crisp bag with a shiver, he decided they were probably gathering together for warmth.

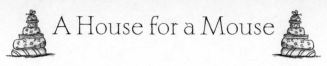 

The mouse had no family and no one to get warm with, so he looked up at the windows of the nearest house and was pleased to see the lights were all switched off. Knowing this meant everyone had gone to bed, he took it as an invitation to go inside and shelter from the snow.

The mouse wriggled through the letterbox and scampered across the carpet into the living room, where he was surprised to find a large tree decorated with coloured lights.

Beneath the tree there were parcels wrapped in patterned paper, and because paper is very good for keeping mice warm in the winter, he tore off two

31

strips and wrapped them around his feet.

The mouse was about to go in search of food when he saw something odd inside the torn parcel, so he lifted it out and held it to the light of the tree. It was a tiny knitted jumper, and he knew what it was for because he'd seen people wearing them.

The jumper was much too small for a person, so he decided it must be for him and pulled it on. It was very warm, so the mouse continued to rip at the parcels and found more tiny clothes, but most of them were dresses and probably not for him.

Then he saw an enormous parcel and ripped a small section of paper away

to find a tiny green door. A few more rips uncovered windows, a chimney, and after a very long time spent climbing and ripping and kicking away scraps of paper, a whole house was revealed!

*This house is just the right size for a mouse to live in*, he thought.

The little mouse opened the door, switched on the lights and then raced around inside exploring all the rooms. The dining room reminded the mouse that he'd not eaten for a while, but although the table was laid out for dinner there was no food on the plates, and after the excitement of all the paper ripping and house exploring, he felt worn out. So he pulled out a chair at the tiny dining table and sat down to rest.

Suddenly the mouse heard a noise and peered through the little window.

In the room outside he could see a pair of black boots in the cold ashes of the fireplace, then a large man dressed in red stepped out and dusted the snowflakes from his shoulders. The mouse froze as the strange man approached the mantelpiece, where someone had left a glass of sherry and a mince pie. He wished he'd seen the mince pie first, but kept perfectly still as the intruder sipped from the glass and took a bite from the pie.

The man in red pulled a small piece of paper from his pocket, read it

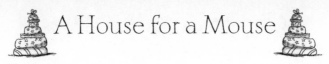 

carefully, and then glanced around the room as though he was looking for something. When he saw the bundles of torn paper he chuckled to himself and headed straight for the little house beside the tree.

The mouse quivered in his seat as the whole front wall of the dining room creaked open like a door and a rosy red face with a long white beard appeared in its place.

"There you are!" The man smiled.

The little mouse looked up guiltily. But instead of chasing him outside with a broom, like most people did, the man broke off a section of mince pie and placed it carefully on the plate in front of him.

"Merry Christmas!" he said and carefully closed the dining room wall.

The mouse was very hungry so he ate the mince pie straight away. It was quite a large portion for such a small creature and took him a while to eat it all. When he'd finished off every crumb, the little mouse moved over to the window and found he was alone again.

The mouse was not sure what to make of the man in red, but after all the unwrapping, and the exploring, and the delicious mince pie, he felt exhausted.

Dawn was already breaking on Christmas Day when the little mouse climbed the stairs in his new little house.

He knew it wasn't really his house, because mice don't live in houses. But he'd had such a nice time and didn't want to return to the crisp bag just yet.

The tired mouse drew the curtains in the bedroom, climbed into bed and wrapped the blanket around him. He didn't mind that he would get chased into the snow later, for now he was happy in a warm little house for a mouse.

So he drifted off to sleep.

Upstairs, Lucy was waking. It wasn't a slow, lazy waking. It was an eager duvet-up-in-the-air waking as she leaped from her bed, pulled on her dressing gown

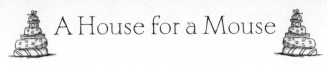 

and burst into her parents' bedroom.

"It's Christmas Day!" she yelled, jumping up and down with excitement.

Lucy's parents opened their drowsy eyes and smiled.

"Can we go downstairs to see if Santa brought my presents?" Lucy asked.

"Of course, darling," yawned her mother. "But I'm sure they're all there. I saw the list you wrote to Santa Claus and I have to say, you really didn't ask for much this year."

"I heard the elves in Santa's workshop built an extra big dolls' house this year, for a very special girl," said her father, with a knowing smile. "And I know for certain that Mrs Claus has been busy making dolls' clothes."

"Oh, I'm sure those things will be there, they were on the main list," said Lucy casually. "But I want to see if Santa Claus got my other letter, the secret one that I didn't tell anyone about."

Lucy's parents immediately sat up in bed. "Another letter?" they gasped.

"Yes, I put my best present on it just to see if Santa Claus was really real," she said. "I addressed it to the North Pole and posted it myself."

Secret glances turned into worried glances as Lucy's parents followed her downstairs. They looked even more worried when they stepped into the living room and found the mess of shredded

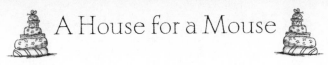 

paper under the Christmas tree.

Lucy ignored the mess, stepped through the torn paper and looked at all the open gifts. Then she took a deep breath and carefully lifted the roof off the dolls' house.

Lucy gasped and clasped her hands over her mouth to stop from shrieking out.

The girl's worried parents rushed to her side and stared into the bedroom of the dolls' house, where a tiny mouse was fast asleep in a miniature bed, wrapped in a miniature blanket.

"Santa Claus *is* real!" Lucy whispered, crouching down and gently stroking the soft furry head of the sleeping mouse.

"I asked him for my very own mouse, to love and to hug and to live in my new dolls' house. And he brought me one!"

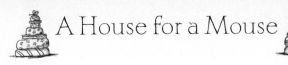 

# THE
# CHRISTMAS
# DRAGON

Vivian French

Old Fox came pattering through the woods, leaving sharp little paw prints in the crisp white snow.

"Coooeeee!" he called. "Are you awake?"

Dragon opened a heavy-lidded eye. Puffs of smoke floated into the air, and over Old Fox's head. Old Fox sneezed.

"I wish you wouldn't do that," he complained. "The smoke gets up my nose."

Dragon opened the other eye. "I *am* a dragon," he said.

Old Fox sneezed twice more. "Well – I suppose you can't help it. At least it keeps things warm round here."

Dragon nodded, and yawned.

"Hey!" Old Fox came closer. "Hey – what are you doing? You're not going back to sleep, are you?"

Dragon sighed, and a flicker of fire sizzled across the snow in front of Old Fox's paws.

"Ooof!" Old Fox jumped back. "Careful!"

Dragon smiled a slow smile. "I'm sorry, old friend. But if you've nothing else to say..." His eyes began to close.

"NO!" Old Fox said sharply. "Listen! I've come specially – I've come to ask you to spend Christmas with us!"

Dragon stirred a little. "Christmas?"

"Yes..." Old Fox waved a paw in the

air. "You know ... twelve days of fun and feasting, jollity, jugglers – all that kind of thing. Holly, carols ... hot dinners..."

"Mmmmm..." Dragon opened his eyes and peered at Old Fox. "Are you up to something?" he asked.

Old Fox looked away, and twirled his whiskers. "What, me? No, no ... we just thought you'd fancy a touch of merriment ... a friendly face or two."

"I was thinking of settling down for a good long rest," Dragon said. "I've never been much in demand around Christmas."

"Not even when it snows?" Old Fox sounded amazed.

"Ahhhh ... so that's it." Dragon

nodded his heavy head.

"What? What do you mean?"

"You're finding the weather cold, Old Fox. You're thinking of warmth ... and flames ... and Christmas fires blazing away..."

"Oh yes!" Old Fox said eagerly. "How did you guess?"

Dragon sighed a long heavy sigh that blew swirls of snow up into the air and sent a spiral of smoke circling round Old Fox, making him cough and splutter.

"A dragon's fire wouldn't be a comfort for a cold fox's toes," Dragon said. "If you're wanting a Christmas blaze you'd be safer collecting twigs and logs and branches..."

Old Fox stroked his nose in a thoughtful way.

"You don't think that a few small puffs and blows might be arranged? Perhaps in return for a wonderful Christmas feast?"

Dragon looked at Old Fox, then turned his head away. He breathed out, a long steady breath. The flames flew high and bright, flaring and flaming against the whiteness of the snow. There was a scorching heat, a crackling, a hissing, and a sizzling. Trees at the edge of the clearing lost their white frosting and turned black and charred. The grass was blackened and burnt as far as Old Fox could see.

"Hmmm." Old Fox coughed.

"Well well well," he said. "Actually – perhaps I should say goodbye now. I think I'll be off to pick up a few sticks, a few seasonal logs…"

He trotted off to the shelter of the trees, and then turned. "Have a good sleep," he said, "and a very happy Christmas."

Dragon smiled. His head sank down between his steely-clawed feet, and he closed his eyes.

It was very quiet.

Dragon lay still, with the stillness of stones, or hills, or slate grey mountains. Wisps of dreams hovered in the air above his head … dreams of sweeping

velvet dresses ... silver gleaming armoured knights ... tall towers casting dark shadows ... the distant beating of horses' hooves ... and while he dreamed, days and weeks and months drifted by.

Not just one Christmas came and went, or two or three or four ... but tens of tens of Christmasses, and tens of tens again and again and again...

and time ticked on...

and on...

and on...

It was bitterly cold. The wind whistled in between the dustbins, shaking and rattling the tins and bottles and scraps of card and paper. Young Fox came hurrying round the corner, shivering. With a rush and a swirl the wind whisked the sprig of holly from behind his ear and tossed it away, and tugged at the small bag of wizened apples and scraps of bread that Young Fox was carrying.

"Brrr," said Young Fox, and paused behind a bin to shelter for a moment. It was warmer than he had expected, and he yawned, and sat down. The warmth crept up to toast his toes and tail. Young Fox's eyes closed, and he curled up into a ball and slept.

It was dark. It was darker than Dragon had ever known darkness to be, and there was a strange heaviness. It

seemed to Dragon that there were hills and forests and mountains pressing down on him. He breathed deeply, and began to stir.

Young Fox let out a terrified howl. The earth was heaving and lifting, and the dustbins fell over and rolled away with a deafening clatter. Smoke and dust swirled in the cold air, and Young Fox was tossed head over heels as the ground rose beneath him. As he staggered back on to his feet he could hear stones rattling and clattering on every side.

Slowly the dust settled, and the smoke cleared.

Young Fox and Dragon looked at

each other, and Young Fox sneezed.

Dragon shook the earth from his nostrils and smiled. "Still sneezing, old friend?" he said.

Young Fox was speechless. He stared and stared at Dragon, his eyes popping.

Dragon yawned, a huge cavernous jagged-toothed yawn.

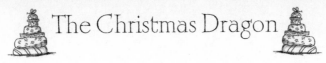 

"I see the snow's gone," he said. "Was it a white Christmas? Did you have your twelve days of holly and hot dinners? Festivals and feasting?"

"We ... we haven't had Christmas yet," Young Fox said, his voice a whisper. "We ... we don't really have that sort of Christmas round here, sir. There's not a lot to have, you see..."

Dragon lowered his huge head to look at Young Fox more closely.

"What? No jollity? No jesting? No feasting?" Dragon blinked his heavy eyelids. He turned, and began to look about him. He saw the tall chimneys, the factories, the dark alleyways, and the long shadows that fell across the clearing.

"Where are the trees?" he asked, his voice deep and rumbling.

Young Fox shifted uneasily from foot to foot. "Er ... I don't think there are any trees round here," he said. "It's been like this as long as I've known it, sir..."

Dragon began to heave his long scaly body up and out of the rubble. Plumes of smoke soared up into the air. Young Fox sneezed, and then coughed.

"Er ... that is, excuse me, sir ... but are you leaving?"

There was a hollow rasping as Dragon unfurled his wings. Young Fox saw they were ragged and tattered and torn.

"I want to bring back the sunshine and the sky," Dragon said, staring angrily

at the tall sooty chimneys that reached up above him.

"Fancy," said Young Fox. "I mean ... won't that be ... that is, isn't that rather difficult?"

Dragon rippled his dusty scales, and flexed his dirty broken claws.

"Once," he said, "a small puff of my breath turned all the trees around this space to blackened ash. One long strong blast of flame, and the way will be clear for them to grow again."

Young Fox jumped up. "WHAT? You mean you could burn all this away? Knock it down?"

Dragon nodded. "One beat of my wings," he said, "and towers will topple."

"But you mustn't!" Young Fox beat his paws against Dragon's steel sides. "You can't – that is, PLEASE, sir – it's where we live!"

Dragon became very still.

"You don't understand–" Young Fox was trembling in his eagerness to explain. "I know it isn't much to a big grand creature like you – just a few bins and things – but we live here, and at Christmas we get together and have a bit of a song and a supper, and we wish each other all the best ... oh, if you could see it, you'd understand, I know you would! OH! Oh – just one moment ..." Young Fox spun round and began scrabbling among the stones. Feverishly

he snatched up as many of the apples and scraps of bread as he could find, and scurrying back he dropped them at Dragon's feet.

"Here!" he said. "Here! You have them! Have them as a very Happy Christmas present from me, and please please PLEASE come and join us tomorrow. We'll all be ever so glad to see you and to share what we've got, although... " he gave his gifts a longing glance, "there may not be much..."

Young Fox's voice died away. Dragon made no move to take the apples or the bread.

He was standing over the clearing, his eyes half closed, his massive bulk unmoving.

61

Young Fox drooped.

"I'm sorry," he said. "What does it matter to you? But you would have liked it ... there's nothing quite like Christmas." And he sighed, and moved towards the darkest of the alleyways.

"One moment, dear friend."

Young Fox stopped. Dragon's voice was gentle, and as Young Fox turned there was a shuddering under his feet as Dragon wearily folded his wings and sank his mountainous body back among the stones.

"You're quite right," Dragon said slowly. "Christmas is not the time for anger, and burning, and destruction. No time at all..." His voice was echoing

hollowly now. "Maybe one day there will be a time for me ... or maybe ... not..."

Dragon's head lay heavily on the tumbled earth. Young Fox saw his eyes close, and, creeping closer, he wondered if he was even breathing. A faint mist hung about him now, and it was difficult for Young Fox to see if Dragon was really there lying in the clearing, or if a heap of rocks and stones and pebbles had fallen into the likeness of a strange and fantastic beast.

The wind blew – a wild gust that picked up the mist and whisked it away. For a moment Young Fox thought he saw an eye flicker in the shadows, but he couldn't be certain. It was growing dark, and thoughts of home and the coming Christmas were tugging at his mind. The wind whistled again, and a small sprig of holly flew into the air and dropped on to the silent mound that lay stone still in the twilight.

Young Fox shivered, and trotted off into the darkness. He hadn't gone far when he stopped, and hurried back.

"It is Christmas," he said as he carefully picked up his scraps and apples. "And they'll be expecting something..." He hopped over a dustbin lid, and saw the sprig of holly. He paused, then shook his head.

"I'll leave it," he said.

The first snowflakes were drifting down as Young Fox pattered down the alleyway that led him home.

"Happy Christmas!" he called over his shoulder. "Happy Christmas!"

# ANITA'S
# CHRISTMAS

Maeve Friel

It was such a frosty evening that Anita's hair was crisp to the touch. She snuggled deeper into her homespun blanket and was just sinking into a deep sleep when the peace was shattered by a loud BOOM!

Something heavy rolled past on rumbling wheels.

An engine roared. A great wind howled.

There were shouts in a foreign language.

"Higher! Higher!"

"Look! There's another."

The long metal arm of the enemy tank advanced, until all her neighbours' homes were crushed and trampled to dust.

There was not a minute to lose, no time to gather up the carefully-wrapped bundles of food that she had prepared earlier. She had to evacuate.

She measured out a long line, counted to ten and jumped.

Looking back over her shoulder, she saw her house being swallowed up in the awful engine's sucking maw.

For several seconds, all her eight legs trembled and her two rows of eyes filled with tears. She scuttled behind the bookcase and rolled herself into a tight ball to wait for the danger to end.

Anita had lived all her life in the same corner of the drawing-room ceiling where she had been born, and where her mother and grandmother had built their webs before her. It was a peaceful place, perhaps a little dull, for the room was not much used by the family, and her spider neighbours kept themselves to themselves on their own webs.

House spiders aren't party animals, unlike the ants that did the conga around the pots on the window sills all summer long.

Sometimes, Anita couldn't help wishing that her life was more exciting, but she couldn't really complain. There was a regular supply of houseflies and wasps and sometimes a moth fluttered by, so she never went hungry. In fact, she was very proud of her pantry, which was always full of ready-to-eat meals rolled up in gossamer packages.

Now, she had lost everything. She would have to start all over again as soon as Mum left, dragging the Weapon of Mass Destruction, or the vacuum cleaner as she called it, behind her. Until then, Anita yawned, she might as well have a little snooze. Spiders need a lot of sleep.

"Careful, mind the vase! Left a bit! No! NOOOO! Too much, back a bit, back a bit, hey, that's my ankle!"

Anita woke with a start.

She crawled out from her hiding-place behind *The Natural History of the Animal Kingdom* and peered down.

Mum and Dad were staggering into the drawing room with a huge fir tree in a pot. They set it down on the right-hand side of the fireplace.

*That's curious!* Anita thought.

She let out a dragline and dropped down to investigate.

Two children came in. She had seen them playing in the garden and knew their names were Jack and Molly.

Jack was carrying a stepladder. Molly was carrying a large box with the words 'Christmas Decorations' written very blackly on the side.

Molly set the box down in front of the tree. Then, she and Jack started to take out golden balls and coloured streamers and red bows and busily set about hanging them on the fir branches. On the very top, they placed a lopsided fairy with a sticky-out dress and two spangly gold wings.

Anita dropped down a little closer.

Dad was on his hands and knees untangling a long cord with little spiky glass tips. After a lot of huffing and puffing and fiddling and muttering, he began to wrap the cord around the tree, starting at the top and twisting and coiling it around and around.

Mum was on the stepladder, looping swags of wine-coloured garlands around the picture rails with sprigs of holly and snow-coloured berries.

At a signal from Dad, Jack and Molly drew the curtains closed. Then he flicked a switch on at the wall.

All the hairs on Anita's legs stood on end. She blinked her two rows of eyes.

The tree lit up!

It gleamed, not like the harsh searchlight that hung in the middle of the ceiling, but with a soft pale golden glow.

She let out more thread and floated away from the sanctuary of the bookcase to have a better look.

It was a bad move.

"AAAARRRGGGHHH!" screamed Jack and Molly and Mum.

"A SPIDER! Kill it, Dad!"

"NO!" protested Dad. He stretched his arms out to shelter Anita. "Leave it alone! It's harmless!"

Anita hung motionless, suspended in mid-air. Everyone was looking at her.

No one had ever *looked* at her before.

She shyly scuttled back up her line and pulled it up behind her.

"Wow!"

"Did you see that?"

"It ran up the thread and pulled it back into its bottom."

"Floating through the air on her flying

trapeze," said Dad.

Jack and Molly looked doubtful.

"Seriously. They have four little organs called spinnerets – more or less on their bottom – that produce a sticky liquid…"

"Yuck!"

"It's not yuck. It's amazing. The spider rubs her hind legs together to gather the liquid into one strong silky line. Then she uses it to build her own house, her web, and to move about on draglines just like this spider was doing. And it's so sticky that she can even trap her prey on it. Actually, it's a good thing she does or the whole world would be overrun with all sorts of creepy-crawlies."

"They're still ugly, though," said Molly, thoughtfully.

"I think she's cute," said Dad. "Look at her long slim elegant legs."

"Hairy legs," added Jack.

"Yes, but those hairs are her ears. She feels sounds vibrating in her hairs. She's probably listening to us right now. And looking at us. They have eight eyes, you know. And they have blue blood. But the very best thing about spiders is that they are artists. The webs they weave are works of art."

Anita swelled with pride. She had no idea! She had blue blood! She was cute! She was an artist!

She let the sticky liquid flow from her

spinnerets, and industriously rubbed her two hind legs together. Then she floated back down again.

She was so happy that she invented a spidery dance. She ascended. She descended. She waved her eight slim elegant hairy legs.

She put her left legs in, she put her right legs out. In, out, she shook them all about. She rolled her two rows of formidable eyes and gnashed her powerful jaws. And as a finale, she somersaulted on her own trapeze so that everyone could see the silky egg sac that she was carrying on her underside.

Molly and Jack giggled. Mum blushed to remember the Weapon of Mass

Destruction. Dad gave Anita a wink.

She sighed. It was so good to have visitors after all those lonely months in her corner. She gave them a spidery smile. She'd show them a web they'd never forget, she decided.

But first, she needed a bit of a lie-down. It had been an exhausting day.

Some time later, Anita was woken by a terrible clattering on the rooftop.

She was all alone in a magic grotto, gleaming with jewel colours. The wine-red garlands looped around the picture rails. The Christmas tree glowed golden by the fireplace with the lopsided fairy still waving her glittery wand. Two furry stockings hung from the mantelpiece where a mug of cocoa and two mince pies were cooling.

Anita shivered and stretched each pair of legs in turn to warm up. It was time to build her new web.

She began in the centre. First she laid out a number of long silk lines like the spokes of a bicycle. Then she daintily began to walk around in bigger and bigger circles, spinning loops of thread and knitting perfect knots at every join.

She was so busy at her work that she didn't even hear the bumping and scraping and "Dearie Me's", coming from the chimney.

It was only when she had completed the final circle and was returning to the hub of her web for a rest that she noticed a pair of black boots had appeared in the grate.

A large red bottom followed. It wiggled and jiggled and crawled out backwards on to the hearth rug, pulling a bulging black sack.

Anita's eight eyes swivelled around to have a better look.

It was a man, dressed in a red suit with white fur trimmings. He stood up, stamped the snow from his boots, and shouted up the chimney.

"It's all right, Rudolph. It was a tight squeeze but I'm in. Tell Donner and

Blitzen and the rest of the reindeer to take five minutes. Jack and Molly have left me some cocoa."

There was a friendly snort in reply.

Father Christmas turned around. His white eyebrows and beard were speckled with soot.

"Hello," he said, saluting Anita with the mug of cocoa. "This is your first Christmas, right? I knew your mother and your grandmother – I can see you're an artist just like them – that's a cracker of a web. Happy Christmas, sweetheart."

And he blew her a kiss.

# Christmas Animal Tales

At first light, the hairs on Anita's legs heard the door creak open.

It was Jack and Molly. They tiptoed in to see what Father Christmas had left for them in their stockings – but what they saw first stopped them in their tracks.

"Oh!"

High up in the corner, above the bookcase, Anita was sitting proudly in the middle of the most perfect, the most artistic, web in the whole world and it was all sparkly and frosty with the breath of Father Christmas's magic Christmas morning kiss.

# LITTLE
# DONKEY

Anna Wilson

My mother called me Little Donkey. I am, and always have been, a very little donkey. When I was born, the others in the stable did not think I would survive more than a few days. But my mother cared for me with a steadfast determination that only comes from true love. She fed me with her sweet milk, and groomed me tenderly. I always felt safe while she was close by.

Every night I would snuggle up to her on our bed of straw and she would tell me stories. She would tell me tales of little donkeys who were braver and wiser than the rest. But still I would worry.

"Mother, why am I so small? I want to be big and strong like the others."

"Little Donkey, dear little one," she would reply. "You don't have to be big to be special."

And I would fall asleep, nestled into her warmth while she softly sang:

*Little donkey, little donkey,*

*on the dusty road.*

*Got to keep on, plodding onwards,*

*with your precious load.*

And then one day her sweet milk disappeared, and I had to eat hay like the others. Shortly after, my mother disappeared too. No one would tell me where she had gone. I missed her and looked for her, but could not find her. With my mother gone, all kindness and sweetness vanished from my life.

At night I would toss and turn on my straw bed which was now too big for me. I cried silent tears and prayed that my mother would come back to me.

One night, I thought she had. I felt a warm nose pushing at me while I slept and jerked up abruptly from my sleep. Mother was standing over me! I was sure it was her. I could smell her sweet breath and her eyes were full of love.

"Little Donkey, dear little one," she said. "Don't cry. Remember what I always told you. You don't have to be big to be special. Sometimes it is the smallest creatures who receive the biggest blessings. You'll see, one day, you'll see, Little Donkey."

I tried to reach up and nuzzle her, to keep her there, standing over me. But she faded from sight.

Life grew hard. The other donkeys started finding new names for me – names that were cruel and harsh – and they kicked me and hoofed me to the back of the queue when the stable boy came to fill the mangers.

"Hee-haw! Hee-haw! Look out, Scrawny!" they would bray.

"No hay for you today, Puny! Hee-haw!"

They would plunge their laughing faces into the mangers and kick me out of the way. To start with, I tried to stick up for myself. I would push and shove back at them and mutter quietly:

"You don't have to be big to be special. Sometimes it is the smallest creatures who receive the biggest blessings."

But they only laughed louder and kicked harder.

After a while I gave up the fight and went out of the stable at mealtimes. I would forage for scratchy thistles and wild grasses outside our master's house; and then I'd trot off to find a quiet spot under a tree where I could stand and chew and dream. The others never noticed I had gone. They were too busy guzzling.

So much for blessings. . .

One hot, dry afternoon, I was munching and dreaming of a brighter future, when my mean master came hurtling towards me from his house. He was cursing and waving his staff in the air.

"You lazy good-for-nothing ass!" he raged. "What are you doing, making a feast of my flowers? You – you—" He struggled to catch his breath as he waddled closer, the better to reach me with his stick.

I ducked out of his way and tried to head back to the stable, baring my teeth and braying in fright. If I could only hide myself in between the other donkeys, the master would not be able to touch me with his hateful staff.

But then a rope was slung around my neck.

"You're coming to market, you pitiful

beast," bellowed the cruel man, as he viciously beat my hindquarters. "I've had enough of feeding a runt like you."

And with my head hanging low and my tail between my legs, I was led away.

The market was a heaving, swollen mass of men and animals, all shouting and stamping and waving and grunting and snorting and braying. I was too frightened to join in the noise. I could do nothing but stand and stare, wide-eyed, at the horrors before me. Animals of all kinds were being beaten and pulled around and yelled at. I could not see what this place was supposed to be. Suddenly, life in my stable seemed cosy and safe.

I turned my head wildly to look for an escape, and found myself face to face with another man: not my master. He was staring at me purposefully, and began stroking my nose in a pleasant, soothing manner.

"There, there, Little Donkey," he was saying, "there, there, little one. There's no need to be frightened."

No one had called me Little Donkey since my mother had gone. The softness in the man's voice reminded me of Mother, too. His eyes were brown with a sparkle in them. I made an effort to steady myself to get a better look at him. His hands were rough and gnarled. Workman's hands, I thought.

Not like the hands of my master which were smooth and pale, and only good for waving sticks at poor donkeys. His clothes, too, were rough and coarse – again, not like my master's.

"Come on, Little Donkey," he said. "You may be small, but you look strong enough."

He led me with a firm but gentle hand, away from the commotion and confusion of the market. We walked on together for many miles. I did not know where I was going, or who this man was. I should have been frightened. But I wasn't.

After hours of walking in the heat and the dust, we stopped outside a small house. The man tied me up and vanished inside. He returned quickly, bearing a bowl of delicious cool water and a bundle of sweet hay. I swiftly looked over my shoulder to see with whom I would be sharing this meal. The man laughed, his brown face creased with amusement.

"It's all for you, Little Donkey! Eat well and rest well. We've a long journey ahead of us," he said.

I did not need any more encouragment to do as he said. That meal was the best I had ever tasted.

☆        ☆        ☆

After a dreamless sleep, the man came to my side and woke me gently.

"Up you get, now, Little Donkey," he whispered. "Time to go."

I staggered to my feet, my eyes blurred with sleep, and shook out my mane. A woman now stood beside the man. Her face was smoother than his, and her skin paler, but she too had kind brown eyes. When she turned to speak to the man, the blue cloak she was wearing fell open, and I saw from the swelling at her belly that she must be with child.

The man bent to whisper in my ear again. "Good Little Donkey," he said. "Good little one."

As he spoke to me, he helped the woman onto my back. No one had ever ridden me before. It should have felt strange. But it didn't.

The man untied the rope that had tethered me to his house, and began to lead me and the woman away. Along the way, he sang in his soothing voice:

# Little Donkey

*Little donkey, little donkey,*

*on the dusty road.*

*Got to keep on, plodding onwards,*

*with your precious load.*

We travelled through the evening and into the night, through little villages and across the sands. At last we came to a small town, just as people were shutting their doors and putting out their lights. The man tried to engage some of the townsfolk in conversation, but they turned from our little group and hurried on, eager to get to their beds.

I too was weary, and yearning for rest, but my new master and mistress had become agitated. I found myself feeling anxious for them, without knowing the reason. They spoke to each other in voices edged with an urgency that I didn't understand.

At last, my master found a man who seemed to have the time to listen.

"Yes, yes, all right," I heard him say. He looked me up and down. "At least your beast is not a large one. You should be comfortable if you don't mind sharing. Just follow me."

I found myself being led into a stable – the first I had seen since leaving my old master. It was warm inside, and there were no other donkeys to kick me and laugh at me. There was an ox at one end, and a manger full of tempting hay.

"Eat well, Little Donkey," said my

master, while he helped my mistress from my back.

When I had had my fill from the manger, my master fetched new hay and lined the manger again. Then he helped my mistress to lie down on the bedding he had brought for her. Exhausted, we settled down together in the warm stable; my master, my mistress and I.

I slept fitfully, my dreams disturbed by cries and shouts and noises that I did not recognize. A searing brightness burst through the stable doors. I awoke with a start, bewildered and scared. A chorus of wondrous music filled the air. I looked out of the stable, into the heavens, and saw that the sky was thronged with terrifying, beautiful creatures, such as I had never seen in my life before.

"Glory to God in the Highest, and on earth, peace to all men!" they cried. "Today in David's town is born a Saviour! And he shall be called Christ the Lord!"

What did this mean? I turned in panic to my master, expecting to see terror written on his face too. But instead I saw him smiling. He was kneeling next to my mistress, and she was smiling also. They were both gazing into the manger.

I trotted towards them, and my master looked up.

"Come, Little Donkey," he said, with

tears of joy in his eyes. "Come and see."

I bent to look into the manger and saw, lying in the hay – a baby! A beautiful baby boy.

I nuzzled his tiny hand. He stirred in his sleep and brushed the tip of my nose with his fingers.

"You have done well, Little Donkey," said a voice.

I looked up and saw my mother standing behind my master.

"Without you, God's son would not have arrived safely. It is as I told you," she said, looking at me, and then at the baby in the manger. "Sometimes it is the smallest creatures who receive the biggest blessings."

# BELL

Penny Dolan

I am Bell. My boy, Nils, gave me that name when he hung the bell around my furry reindeer neck.

"My grandfather made it," my boy told me. "That is what old Anya says."

My bell was the sweetest bell in all the herd, but reindeer games can be rough, and so it got broken. Now it hangs silently around my neck.

Nils has no bell round his neck. He lives with old Anya. She looks after him, and he looks after me.

He wears an old fur-lined coat Anya cut down to fit him, and a cap with flaps to keep his ears warm. Though he looks fat as a bear-cub, his face is thin. He and Anya have to make do with what they can get.

Old Anya and Nils have worked hard helping around the village, for every home must be ready for the winter feast. It takes no longer than a shake of my tail for Nils to bring green branches and Anya to place a fresh candle in the window of their hut. They are as ready as they can be.

Nils comes running across the glistening snow to greet me.

"Here, Bell!" He holds out a handful of dried moss.

"It tastes green as spring," I tell him, though he only pretends to understand reindeer speech. Nils leans his head against me. "Boy, what is it?" I ask.

"Everyone is kind, Bell. They give Anya things they do not need," he sighs, "but I do wish I could have something new, something of my very own."

The herd has wandered away, and Nils and I are alone. A bright light is coming closer through the darkness. It is a tall hooded stranger holding a lantern. I immediately lower my antlers as a warning.

The man wears a long red robe. He cannot have walked very far in such clothes. How has he got here?

# Bell

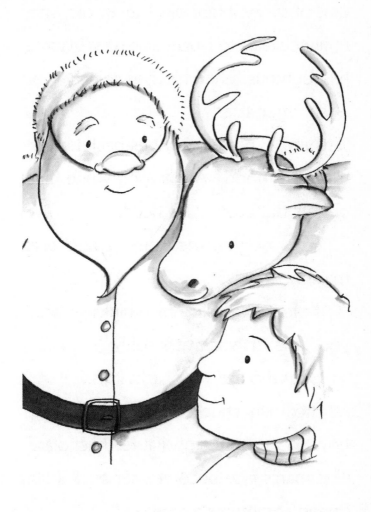

His beard falls across his chest like a drift of snow. He looks like an old one, until he starts to laugh, as if he is glad he has found us. Then his eyes shine young as summer skies.

"Nils?" The man pushes back his fur-trimmed hood. A halo of white hair bushes out around his head.

"How do you know my name?" says my boy.

"I often hear old Anya thinking about you," the man answers softly.

"But who are you?" asks Nils.

The man chuckles quietly. "Tonight, boy, you can call me Father Nicholas." The man's face becomes serious. "Nils, I need something from you."

Nils points back to the village. "Not me. I have nothing to give," he says. "Try over there. They will probably have what you need."

The man pats my muzzle, and runs a firm hand along my fur. "No, young Nils. You have what I need. I have to make a journey, and one of my reindeer has gone lame. May I borrow Bell for one night?"

Nils frowns. I am the only thing he owns. "Is it a long journey?"

"Yes, Nils, and a hard one. But Bell will be back with you by morning."

Nils looks at the man, and then at me. "You can take Bell," he says at last, "but you must take me too. Then we will both be back by morning."

The man looks into my boy's eyes, and pauses a moment. "Then that is what I shall promise!" he laughs.

Nils smiles, but I am not sure about this adventure. I prance about anxiously, and kick up the snow.

"Come, Bell! There will never be a night like tonight, my friend," he says, and something in his voice makes me trust him.

His sledge is in a clearing among the trees. It seems magnificent, grand enough for an emperor, although the red velvet cushions have faded to a rusty rose, and the runners show signs of many long journeys.

The sledge is loaded with sacks. I

sniff. There is no smell of hay or pine-cones, or bread or meat. Nothing important. The scent is of spices and honey.

"Time is precious tonight," the man says, and he fastens Nils safely and warmly into the seat.

"Look!" my boy gasps.

Seven reindeer appear in front of the strange sledge. The tips of their antlers sparkle like frost, and their eyes are deep and wise. They do not smell like my own herd, but I sense no danger.

The oldest deer wears a huge crown of silvery antlers. He turns his mighty head. "Greetings, Bell," he says. "You are welcome to fly with us tonight."

"Greetings!" I reply, bowing my head, and scraping the ground politely with my hoof. Fly? What a strange word to use! Does he mean race? I have never raced with creatures like these!

The man leads me towards the empty space in the team. He buckles the straps, and calms me with a pat.

"My brave Bell, you look so perfect there that I nearly forgot," he laughs gently. His cheeks are as red as apples.

"Forgot what?" I wonder.

He reaches deep into his pocket, and sprinkles a handful of silvery dust along my back and across my hooves. I feel as if a strong wind is riffling through my fur.

"Why did he do that?" I ask the other

reindeers. Their laughter makes white clouds in the cold night air.

"You will find out," says the oldest. "But do not be afraid."

"Ready, my friends?" the man calls. "Ready, Bell? Ready, young Nils? Let's go!"

As he tugs the reins, small bells start to jingle. Soon the loaded sledge moves more smoothly. I cannot see Nils, tucked away behind me. All I see are the hooves of the reindeers ahead, and their silvery antlers. We run, we race, across the snow faster and faster, faster and faster.

"Keep going, friends!" the man cries as we speed along. "Up, up, up!"

All at once, I cannot feel the ground beneath me, not at all. We are moving up, high into the sky. We are flying, we are!

The midnight moon makes a path for us across the rolling water. We travel far and fast. My own land is far behind. My hooves are dancing on the wind, and I am full of joy.

This is when something most mysterious happens. It is as if, for this single night of nights, time passes more than once.

I feel as if we are flying endlessly, never stopping, always whirling through the sky. The sledge is crossing mountains and valleys, deserts and plains, rivers and oceans. I feel as if we are running the whole wide world round without a stop.

Yet, at the very same moment, sometimes I am convinced our hooves are on roof-slates, or thatch or even the grassy ground. Father Nicholas is calling at each home. This is strange too, for I can see both outside and inside.

He is there, climbing down a waiting chimney. He is there, by trees shimmering with decorations. He is there, sprinkling his magic so that the packages sparkle with happiness. He is there, taking gifts from his sacks, and showering handfuls of magic over all he finds.

As his red-robed figure passes through the rooms, he whispers. Even though the words are different, and I cannot hear all he says, the sleeping people smile as if they hear the same message.

"Joyeux Noël! God Jul! Fröhliche Weihnachten! Wesolych Swiat Bozego Narodzenia! Feliz Navidad!"

Sometimes – or am I dreaming this too? – we reindeers are resting, munching carrots and apples. It is hard to believe this night is happening.

We pass over foxes in fields, and wild woods where wolves prowl. We circle over cities so full of light nobody sees us flying overhead. We swoop low, alongside a building with spires and windows of coloured glass.

"See, Nils," the man says.

Inside is a small, small stable. Tiny carved shepherds stand with their sheep, and a tiny carved man and woman gaze at a tiny baby. Nearby, three tiny wooden kings bring gifts. Suddenly, the night fills with loud ringing bells, and people singing as if they are sharing their hopes.

"Time to go," says the man, and we are off again.

As northern lights flicker across the sky, down, down, down we go.

The man carries my deep-asleep boy indoors and places him gently into his bed. Then he lays two gifts down by the hearth, for Anya and for Nils.

As he unbuckles the harness, and sets

me free, the man says, "You did well. I would never have reached Christmas Day without your help."

I stare at the man. Christmas Day? Is this what my great race was for?

"Yes," he answers, as if he knows my mind. "Thank you, Bell."

Father Nicholas playfully taps at the bell around my neck. Suddenly, it rings out again, clear and bright! I shake my head, making the bell sing out joyfully again.

Then I look up, but the man and his reindeer are gone.

# THE
# KITTEN TREE

Holly Webb

"Come on, girls! Emily, what are you bringing that for?"

"I want to show him to Grandma." Five-year-old Emily had her favourite present, a two-metre-long cuddly snake called George, wrapped round her neck like a fat and dangerous scarf.

"Emily, we're walking to Grandma's." Molly knelt down by her little sister. "George is heavy. You'll get tired carrying him. And he might get dirty if you drop him."

"I want to show George to Grandma!" Emily's face was going red. Her family knew the signs, so Molly shrugged. "I'll help her carry him."

Mum nodded. No one wanted an Emily tantrum on Christmas Day. She could go on for ages, and the girls' grandma was expecting them. "All right, if we must."

Dad took Emily's hand, and tucked a box of crackers under his arm. "Ready, everyone? Come on, Emily, let's go and see if Grandma's got a present for you."

Emily nodded happily, and started to pull him towards the door. "Maybe she's got me another snake!" she was squeaking excitedly.

Mum and Molly looked at each other and sighed.

Ruby the kitten stretched and yawned luxuriously. She was draped along the back of the sofa, snoozing after a big lunch. It had been particularly good, with turkey, and gravy. Emily had tried to feed her something called Christmas pudding as well, but Molly had stopped her. Ruby hadn't minded. It hadn't smelled like her kind of thing anyway. She could still smell turkey though. Mmmm… She wondered if they'd put it all away in the fridge?

Suddenly Ruby sat bolt upright. They'd all gone for mince pies at

# The Kitten Tree

Grandma's house! This was her moment. For the last two weeks, Ruby had been desperate to investigate the Christmas tree. It was so clearly meant for kittens to climb, but no one seemed to want her to. They kept shooing her away. Ruby leaped delicately down from the sofa, and padded over to the tree, whiskers twitching in excitement. She sat in front of it, curling her tail around her paws thoughtfully. Where should she start? She reached out and batted a silver bauble, which swung deliciously. She batted it again, a little harder, but this time it came off, thudding onto the floor. Ruby peered down at it, wondering if it would bounce up again.

She jumped back, fur bristling, when she saw another cat inside, one with a strange wide face, enormous eyes and silvery tabby stripes like hers. She hissed, and the other cat made a hissy face, but no noise came out. It seemed well and truly stuck in there. Good. This was *her* house.

Ruby had been hoping not to leave any evidence of her climb, so she scooted the bauble, and the trespassing cat, under the sofa.

The cat intruder had been a little bit of a shock. Obviously, for an expedition up a Christmas tree, a kitten's nerves needed to be in top working order. Ruby took up a guarding position on the sofa arm, just in case that cat tried coming out again, and settled down for a good wash.

Ten minutes later, Ruby was ready to try again. She peeked under the sofa, but the other cat was still underneath, and didn't seem to see her. Her tail held proudly high, Ruby strutted over to the

Christmas tree. If there were any more cats hiding in it, they had better watch out! This time, she didn't let herself get distracted by swinging baubles – she was looking for the way up. Ever since the girls' father had carried the Christmas tree into the house, Ruby had wanted to get inside it and explore, and when they'd added tinsel and twinkly lights and a fairy doll on the top, it just got even more interesting.

Ruby stood up with her paws on the big, gold-painted pot that Mum and Molly had made. She shook her ears twitchily as a few pine needles pattered down around her. There were a lot of branches, but none of them looked very secure. She tested one lightly with a paw. More pine needles whispered down. Hmmm. Ruby was only a few months old, but she'd learned a lot in that time, and one of the most important things she knew was that a Big Leap was often the answer. She jumped for the biggest branch she could see, scrabbling her soft, shiny little claws at it. But it wasn't there! Or, actually, the branch was there, it was Ruby that wasn't. She was on the floor, blinking dazedly up at the tree. The twinkly lights seemed to be shimmering even more than before, and moving about. And there might have been another cat in one of those baubles, laughing at her.

Ruby was forced to consider something that she hadn't thought of before. Was it possible that the tree did not want her to climb it? No, that was silly. She knew trees. There were trees in her garden, and she climbed those. They didn't mind. But then this was an indoor tree. Maybe indoor trees were fussy? Ruby stood up and glared at the tree. It was in her house, therefore it was her tree. That was obvious. So it was going to be climbed, whether it liked it or not. Perhaps not a Big Leap, though, that method hadn't been quite as successful as she had hoped.

Cautiously, she hooked some tinsel with one claw, and pulled. The tinsel sagged, but not too much. It wasn't going to be much good to climb on though, too thin and straggly. And it stuck to her claws, uugh! Ruby shook her paw hard, and the tangled tinsel yanked away from the tree and managed to wrap itself around her several times. It was alive! And it was attacking her!

Ruby and the tinsel wrestled for a good five minutes until she was happy that it was thoroughly beaten. Then she stepped daintily out of the nest of sparkly shredded silver bits, and had another reassuring wash, paying particular attention to her poor paws. Once they were back to their old selves, Ruby turned again to the tree, a determined gleam in her eyes. This time, she meant business. It was now clear to her that she'd been distracted by silly things like tinsel and feathery branches. Trees had trunks, and that was what she needed. She would wriggle her way up the trunk.

A very small doubt had begun to grow in the back of Ruby's mind. It was all very well getting up the tree, but what was she going to do when she was there? Was there any point to all this? Might it not be better to go back to the sofa and have a bit more of a sleep instead? Ruby squashed the doubt firmly back down. She had been planning to climb the Christmas tree for ages. She didn't need a reason. It was just a kitten thing.

# The Kitten Tree

This was clearly a sneaky tree, so Ruby needed to be sneaky too. She settled into her hunting pose, tummy to the carpet, and crept round to the back of the tree. Ruby had done lots of hunting. She'd never actually caught anything, but that wasn't important. The tree was going to get a big shock. She'd be at the top before it knew what had hit it. She launched herself on to the pot, and swarmed as fast as she could up the tree trunk, her eyes like slits and her ears laid back. The pine needles were showering all round her, but she wasn't going to stop.

Amazingly enough, it worked. Ruby was quite surprised, although, of course, she pretended she'd known she could do it all along. She clung to the top of the tree, peering triumphantly round the fairy doll's sparkly skirt. It was wonderful! She could see everything: the sofa, the table, Molly and Emily's piles of new toys and books. The floor . . . which seemed to be an awfully long way down. Ruby tightened her grip on the tree. She was still wobbling, though. The tree was wobbling her. In fact, one might even say it was swaying. The floor definitely was a very long way down. Down wasn't something that Ruby had really planned for.

What would happen if she just let go? Ruby tried, but her claws wouldn't do it.

They seemed to think it was Not A Good Idea. Could she go back the same way she had come? Nose first? Ruby leaned over to look, and the top of the tree came too, and the fairy doll. Then they all bounced back again, rather hard.

When the tree had stopped swinging – almost – Ruby took a deep breath. Maybe down wasn't a good place to be at the moment. She would stay with up, until...

# Christmas Animal Tales

Aha! There were noises in the hallway. Ruby tried to look as relaxed as anyone could while clinging for dear life to the top of a Christmas tree.

"Ruby!" Molly called. "We're back! Do you want some tea? More turkey? Ruby, where are you?"

"Mrowl!" Ruby spat back crossly. Of course she wanted tea, but she was a bit busy at the top of a tree at the moment, actually…

Molly popped her head round the door and gasped. Then she raced back into the hallway, while Ruby hissed furiously after her. "Where are you going? Get me down!"

Molly was back seconds later with

Dad running behind. "I knew we should have shut her in the kitchen," he groaned. "I wonder how long she's been up there. Come on, you silly cat." And he reached up and grabbed Ruby round the middle. It wasn't very dignified, but she decided not to complain this time. At least Molly made a proper fuss of her, stroking her till Ruby closed her eyes and purred happily. After a little more petting, she opened her eyes again, staring thoughtfully over Molly's shoulder at the curtains. She hadn't really noticed them before.

They looked as though they might be fun to climb. . .

# TALKING
# TURKEY

by Alan Durant

Once there was a turkey called DA760/5/Y. Well, that's what it said on the tag around his leg. All the turkeys on the farm had tags but DA760/5/Y was different in one very special way: he could talk. And not just turkey talk – like gobble gobble gobble – but real proper human talk. In fact not only could he talk, but he could read and write as well! *But how could that be?* I hear you ask. How could a turkey possibly talk and read and write? Well, all I can say in reply is "I haven't the faintest idea." That's just the way it was. From the moment he hatched out of his egg, he could talk. And if you don't believe me, well, that's your problem.

Now, the farmer had no idea that he had such an extraordinary bird among his flock, because DA760/5/Y didn't make use of his amazing gift. The farmer and his men didn't say much when they were around the turkeys – they just shouted at them now and then and called them rude names, which DA760/5/Y understood very well but thought it better to ignore. He just went on with his turkey life – which wasn't terribly interesting to be honest.

# Christmas Animal Tales

The turkeys all lived in a gloomy shed and did little more than strut when they could, eat and chatter – gobble gobble gobble, etc. And turkey conversation, I have to tell you, is not the most fascinating that you will ever hear.

"I stepped on a bit of poo this morning."

"Oh, really, I did that yesterday."

No, life in the turkey shed was not very exciting.

But one day all that changed.

It was a chilly December morning and DA760/5/Y was in the turkey shed with the other birds. He was thinking about a new word he had heard one of the farmer's men say the previous day (he loved hearing new words!). The word was twizzler. What on earth could it mean, he wondered? And what did it have to do with turkeys? "Turkey twizzlers" the man had said. Was it another insult?

Just then the shed door opened and there was the farmer and one of his men with buckets of feed for the turkeys' breakfast. What a noise the turkeys made! You would have thought they hadn't been fed for a week – though most of them, it has to be said, were so fat they could barely stand up and could have done with missing a few meals. DA760/5/Y was one of the few who could still strut without falling over.

"There you are, my tubbies," said the farmer, as he poured out the feed. "Tuck in and eat yourselves silly."

"I think they're well past that," laughed his helper. "Still, they are looking nice and plump."

"Mmm," agreed the farmer, rubbing his hands together. "They'll make a fine price at market for us and excellent Christmas dinners for our customers. Everyone's a winner."

"Except the turkeys," said the man with a sly smile. "Who'd be a turkey at Christmas, eh?" he laughed.

"Oh, they don't know any better," said the farmer. "When we put them in the truck for the slaughterhouse tomorrow, they'll still be gabbling away like they were off on holiday." He chuckled too. Then he showed the other man a piece of paper. "What do you think of my promotional leaflet?" he asked.

"Sizzling," said the man and they both laughed again. Then the two men picked up their buckets, shut the door and left the turkeys to their eating.

Well, I'm sure you won't be surprised to hear that DA760/5/Y had no appetite at all. He was shocked and appalled, as he considered what he had just heard. They were going to be sold! They were going to be Christmas dinners! And he didn't know what a slaughterhouse was but it didn't sound nice at all! Something had to be done – and fast.

"Brother and sister turkeys, listen to me!" he cried. "I have something important to tell you!"

"Oh shush," gobbled one particularly

fat turkey, known to the other turkeys as Gobbler. "You're interrupting our breakfast."

"Never mind breakfast," said our hero. "If you don't pay attention to me you're going to be someone's dinner!"

The others turkeys laughed at that.

"What are you talking about?" said one.

"Your head is full of nonsense," said another.

"No, it's true!" DA760/5/Y insisted. "I heard the farmer say so. Tomorrow they are taking us in a truck to a place called a slaughterhouse to be sold and then we're going to be Christmas dinners."

"Of course we're going away," said Gobbler. "We turkeys always go away at Christmas. We get in a truck and go off on our holiday. Every turkey knows that. Slaughter House must be the name of the resort they're taking us to."

"I hope it has one of those nice water troughs to splash in," said another. "I love those."

"Mmm water troughs!" gobbled the other turkeys excitedly. As you can see, it doesn't take much to get a turkey excited.

"Forget water troughs!" hissed DA760/5/Y in exasperation. "If we get in that truck, we're going to die!"

But still the other turkeys wouldn't listen to him.

Then suddenly DA760/5/Y saw something by the shed door: it was a piece of paper. Quickly DA760/5/Y strutted over and picked it up in his beak. It was the leaflet the farmer had been showing his helper. "Make your Christmas sizzle with Farmer Kelly's turkeys!" it read. "The tastiest turkeys you could ever wish for." Underneath was a picture of a brown, roasted turkey in a dish, surrounded by vegetables. DA760/5/Y gulped.

"What is it?" gobbled Gobbler. "What's the matter?"

"This," said DA760/5/Y and he showed the others the leaflet. The response wasn't what he expected.

"Ooh, nice," said one turkey.

"Lovely looking vegetables," said another.

"What's that brown thing?" asked a third.

DA760/5/Y sighed and shook his head. "Don't you see?" he said. "It's a turkey! That's what they're going to do to us."

Once again the other turkeys laughed, though more nervously this time.

"Don't be silly," said Gobbler. "How can that be a turkey? Where's its head?"

"They cut it off," replied DA760/5/Y, "just like they're going to cut off yours." This statement was met by gabbles of dismay, which only increased when DA760/5/Y read out what was written on the leaflet. Suddenly the shed squawked and flapped with panic: "We're going to die! Our heads are coming off! They're going to sizzle us!"

It was a while before DA760/5/Y managed to get some calm again. But that gave him some time to think. "Don't worry," he said when the other turkeys had stopped gabbling. "I have a plan."

The next morning, when the farmer opened the shed door, he got a big surprise. Turkeys rushed and wobbled out at him in an angry flurry of beak and wing and claw. They drove him and his helper back into the farmyard. Then the turkeys formed a circle around the shed. DA760/5/Y meanwhile flew up onto the roof and perched there.

The farmer's surprise turned to utter astonishment when DA760/5/Y started speaking to him. Well, imagine how you'd feel if a turkey suddenly started talking to you.

"Farmer Kelly," said DA760/5/Y in a cool, clear voice, "we know what you plan for us turkeys – and we protest." He held up the leaflet. "Turkeys are not just for Christmas. We are creatures not twizzlers (he had found this word explained in the leaflet and was very pleased to be able to use it for the first time now), and we have the right to live."

Gobbler, the fat turkey, had no idea what DA760/5/Y was saying but he thought it might be something to do with getting extra food, so he fluffed up his tail feathers and pushed himself forward to draw the farmer's attention. Unfortunately, he was so fat that he fell over. The farmer didn't notice, though. He just stood in silence, gawping at DA760/5/Y, with his helper beside him.

"Well, what do you say?" DA760/5/Y demanded.

The farmer swallowed. "Y-y-y-y-y-y-y-ou can talk," he stammered at last.

"I can," DA760/5/Y confirmed.

"Can you all talk?" asked the farmer.

"Only me," DA760/5/Y replied.

"A talking turkey," murmured the other man, as if he didn't believe it.

"Wh-what is it you want?" said the farmer.

"Bring me a pen and paper and I shall write down my demands," said DA760/5/Y.

The farmer brought the pen and paper. He couldn't wait to see DA760/5/Y write. A talking turkey was one thing, but a turkey that could write. Why, that was more than most of his helpers could do!

DA760/5/Y rested his left claw on

the paper, took the pen in his right
claw and started to write:

Our Demands.
We are to be treated
with respect.
We are not to be sold to
anyone (without our consent).
We are not to be taken to
the slaughterhouse.
We are not to be eaten at
Christmas (or any other
time).
We are not to be called
twizzlers.
Signed
DA760/5/r
On behalf of the turkeys

The farmer looked at the paper – and he looked at DA760/5/Y.

"Good writing," he said, "for a turkey."

"Thank you," said DA760/5/Y.

"I'll have to think about this," said the farmer. "Why don't you all go back and wait in the shed."

DA760/5/Y smiled and shook his head. He was no fool. "No way," he said. "We're staying right here."

"Gobble gobble gobble," added the other turkeys, which I'd like to tell you made sense, but it didn't. It meant, "We've stepped on poo and we will again." As you've already gathered, they weren't the brightest birds in the coop.

The farmer went away with the turkeys' demands. He had no intention of meeting them, but he needed some time to think. He thought over lunch (turkey twizzlers and chips) and he thought over tea (turkey sandwiches and jelly). He knew that a talking turkey could make him very rich – people would come from far and wide to see such a bird.

But, and it was a big but (and I'm not talking about his bottom – though that was big too), this talking turkey and his demands for turkey rights would put him out of business. It would put every turkey farmer out of business and he couldn't allow that. And what about all those disappointed customers with no sizzling Christmas dinner to enjoy? No, the truck had arrived to take his turkeys to the slaughterhouse and that was what it was going to do. He'd just have to shoot that talking turkey. So, after tea, he took his shotgun  and walked out into the yard…

Now, you're probably thinking, this isn't good. The story shouldn't end this way with the hero getting his head shot off and all the other turkeys going to the slaughterhouse. What sort of Christmas story is that? But, that's life for you. It can't always have a happy ending. Not even at Christmas.

# Talking Turkey

☆　　　☆　　　☆

However, don't fret because this story does have a happy ending. When the farmer went out into the yard, it was full of people: children, adults, newspaper reporters – there was even a TV camera crew. *Where did they all come from?* I hear you ask. And it's a very sensible question. Let me explain. The farmer's children had seen and heard the talking turkey as they were on their way to school. Well, of course, they told their friends. Their friends told their friends. Their friends didn't really have any friends, but they told their parents. Word quickly got around about this amazing talking turkey, and now everyone had come to see.

Well, the farmer could hardly shoot DA760/5/Y now. No, DA760/5/Y was saved. He became a celebrity and signed lots of autographs. (I'm afraid I can't tell you what happened to the other turkeys, though I expect they went on a sizzling holiday somewhere.) Everyone wanted to hear the amazing talking turkey's story and interview him. After a while, DA760/5/Y even got his own chat show on TV, called *Talking Turkey*. You may have seen it. He talks to guests about important bird issues of the day. And at the end of every programme he signs off by looking into camera and saying his famous catchphrase, "This is DA760/5/Y saying gobble gobble goodnight and remember, folks, a turkey isn't just for Christmas!"

# Lost in the Snow

Holly Webb

Illustrated by Sophy Williams

Fluff is desperate to have a home of her own like her brothers and sisters – but no one seems to want her. . .

Then Ella turns up at the farm. She falls in love with Fluff straight away and pleads with her mother to let her have Fluff, but her mother is firm – they don't want a cat.

Fluff and Ella are heartbroken . . . and Fluff is terrified. What happens to kittens that nobody wants?

# Lost in the Storm

Holly Webb

Illustrated by Sophy Williams

Ella loves her kitten, Fluff, and worries
about her going missing again. But Fluff
enjoys the freedom of being outside,
especially when it starts snowing and she
has the pretty snowflakes to play with
and lots of wintry gardens to explore.

But suddenly a blizzard sets in and Fluff
can't find her way home. Will Ella ever
be reunited with her kitten?

# Alfie All Alone

Holly Webb

Illustrated by Sophy Williams

Evie is overjoyed when she is given her very own puppy, Alfie. Alfie adores Evie – he loves to be cuddled, sleeps on her bed and welcomes her home from school every day with a wag of his tail.

But it's not long before another new member of the family arrives: Evie's baby brother, Sam. Suddenly no one has much time to look after Alfie, let alone play with him and take him for walks, and soon he finds himself unwanted and all alone. . .

# Animal Rescue

Tina Nolan

Abandoned … lost … neglected…?
There's always a home at Animal Magic!

In a perfect world there'd be no need for
Animal Magic. But Eva and Karl
Harrison, who live at the animal rescue
centre with their parents, know that life
isn't perfect. Every day there's a new
arrival in need of their help!

# Book One

# Honey
## The unwanted puppy

When Eva finds Honey, a beautiful golden retriever puppy, dumped on the doorstep of Animal Magic, she's desperate to find the lovable dog a new home. But Karl has other ideas ... he wants to follow up the clue to find Honey's real owner...

# Book Two

# Charlie
## The home-alone kitten

Everything's going well for Animal
Magic's Open Day, until celebrity guest,
soccer star Jake Adams, cancels at the last
minute. Eva turns detective, but when
she arrives at Jake's house all she finds is
his ginger kitten, Charlie, locked out
and miaowing on the doorstep...

# Book Three

# Merlin
## The homeless foal

When Merlin the foal is born at Animal
Magic, Eva is desperate for him to be
re-homed nearby. But it seems as if he
will be moved to a farm too far away for
her to visit. And that's not all Eva has to
worry about: Mrs Brooks's plan to close
down the rescue centre looks set to
become a reality...

# Book Four

# Rusty
## The injured fox cub

When Eva discovers an injured fox cub down by the river she's desperate to nurse him back to health. Eva can't help picking him up and cuddling him even though her mum has warned her that Rusty isn't a pet. Has Eva's love ruined Rusty's chance of being returned to the wild?

# Book Five

# Bella
## The runaway rabbit

When Bella the baby rabbit arrives
at the Animal Magic rescue centre,
she's terrified of humans and hides
at the back of her hutch. Can Eva
help Bella to make friends?